'There sat the dog with eyes as big as mill wheels.'

HANS CHRISTIAN ANDERSEN
Born 1805, Odense, Denmark
Died 1875, Copenhagen

ANDERSEN IN PENGUIN CLASSICS
Fairy Tales

HANS CHRISTIAN ANDERSEN

The Tinderbox

Translated by
Tiina Nunnally

PENGUIN BOOKS

PENGUIN CLASSICS

UK | USA | Canada | Ireland | Australia
India | New Zealand | South Africa

Penguin Books is part of the Penguin Random House group of companies
whose addresses can be found at global.penguinrandomhouse.com.

This selection published in Penguin Classics 2015
006

Translation copyright © Tiina Nunnally, 2004

The moral right of the translator has been asserted.

Set in 9/12.4 pt Baskerville 10 Pro
Typeset by Jouve (UK), Milton Keynes
Printed in Great Britain by Clays Ltd, St Ives plc

A CIP catalogue record for this book is available from the British Library

ISBN: 978–0–141–39804–4

www.greenpenguin.co.uk

MIX
Paper from
responsible sources
FSC® C018179

Penguin Random House is committed to a
sustainable future for our business, our readers
and our planet. This book is made from Forest
Stewardship Council® certified paper.

Contents

The Tinderbox

A soldier came marching along the road: left, right! left, right! He had his knapsack on his back and a sword at his side, because he had been off to war, and now he was on his way home. Then he met an old witch on the road. She was so hideous, her lower lip hung all the way down to her breast. She said, 'Good evening, soldier. What a nice sword and big knapsack you have – you must be a real soldier! Now you shall have all the money you could ask for!'

'Well, thanks a lot, you old witch,' said the soldier.

'Do you see that big tree?' said the witch, pointing at a tree right next to them. 'It's completely hollow inside. Climb up to the top and you'll find a hole that you can slip into and slide all the way down inside the tree. I'll tie a rope around your waist so I can hoist you back up when you call me.'

'Why would I go inside that tree?' asked the soldier.

'To get the money!' said the witch. 'You see, when you reach the bottom of the tree, you'll be in a huge passageway that's very bright because it's lit by more than a hundred lamps. Then you'll see three doors, and you'll be able to open them because the keys are in the locks. If you go inside the first chamber you'll see a big chest in the middle of the room, and on top of it sits a dog. He has eyes as big as a pair of teacups, but never mind that. I'll give you my blue-checked apron that you can spread on the floor. Go right over and pick up the dog and set him on my apron. Then open the chest and take as many *skillings* as you like. They're all made of copper, but if you'd rather have silver, then go into the next room. In there is a dog with eyes as big as a pair of mill wheels, but never mind that. Set him on my apron and take the money. But if it's gold you want, you can have that too, and as much as you can carry, if you go into the third chamber. But the dog sitting on the money chest has two eyes that are each as big as the Round Tower. Now that's a real dog, believe me! But never you mind. Just set him on my apron and he won't harm you. Then take from the chest as much gold as you like.'

'Not bad,' said the soldier. 'But what do I have to give you in return, you old witch? Because I imagine there must be something you want.'

'No,' said the witch, 'I don't want a single *skilling*. All you have to bring me is an old tinderbox that my grandmother left behind when she was down there last.'

'Fine. Then let's have that rope around my waist,' said the soldier.

'Here it is,' said the witch. 'And here is my blue-checked apron.'

So the soldier climbed up the tree, tumbled down the hole, and then, just as the witch had said, he stood inside the huge passageway where hundreds of lamps were burning.

He opened the first door. Ooh! There sat the dog with eyes as big as teacups, staring at him.

'You're a handsome fellow!' said the soldier and set him

on the witch's apron. Then he took as many copper *skillings* as his pockets would hold, closed the chest, put the dog back, and went into the second room. Eeek! There sat the dog with eyes as big as mill wheels.

'You shouldn't look at me so hard,' said the soldier. 'You might hurt your eyes!' And then he set the dog on the witch's apron, but when he saw all the silver coins inside the chest he threw away the copper coins he was carrying and filled his pockets and his knapsack with nothing but silver. Next he went into the third chamber. Oh, how hideous! The dog in there really did have eyes as big as round towers, and they were spinning around in his head like wheels.

'Good evening,' said the soldier and doffed his cap, for he had never seen a dog like that before. But after he'd looked at him for a while, he thought to himself, 'All right, that's enough.' And he lifted him onto the floor and opened the chest. Good Lord, there was a lot of gold! Enough to buy all of Copenhagen and every single sugar-pig sold by the cake-wives, and all the tin soldiers, whips, and rocking horses in the whole world! Yes, there was certainly plenty of money! So the soldier threw away all the silver coins that filled his pockets and knapsack and took the gold instead. Yes, all his pockets, his knapsack, his cap, and his boots were so full that he could hardly walk. Now he had money! He put the dog back on the chest, slammed the door shut, and called up through the tree:

'Hoist me up now, you old witch!'

'Do you have the tinderbox?' asked the witch.

'Oh, that's right,' said the soldier. 'I forgot all about it.'

And he went over and picked it up. The witch hoisted him up and he once again stood on the road, with his pockets, boots, knapsack, and cap full of money.

'What do you want the tinderbox for?' asked the soldier.

'That's none of your business,' said the witch. 'You've got the money. Now just give me the tinderbox.'

'Pish posh!' said the soldier. 'Tell me right now what you want it for or I'll pull out my sword and chop off your head!'

'No,' said the witch.

So the soldier chopped off her head. There she lay! But he wrapped up all his money in her apron, slung it in a bundle over his shoulder, stuffed the tinderbox in his pocket, and headed straight for the city.

It was a lovely city, and he went inside the loveliest of inns and demanded the very best rooms and his favorite food, because now he had so much money that he was rich.

The servant who was supposed to polish his boots thought they were rather strange old boots for such a rich gentleman to be wearing, but he hadn't yet bought himself new ones. By the next day he had a good pair of boots and fine clothes to wear. The soldier was now a distinguished gentleman, and the people told him about all the splendid things to be found in their city, and about their king and what a charming princess his daughter was.

'Where might I catch a glimpse of her?' asked the soldier.

'It's impossible to catch a glimpse of her,' they all said. 'She lives in an enormous copper palace surrounded by dozens of walls and towers. No one but the king dares visit her, because it was foretold that she would marry a simple soldier, and that certainly did not please the king.'

'She's someone I'd like to see,' thought the soldier, but that wasn't possible.

He was now leading a merry life, going to the theater, taking drives in the king's gardens, and giving away a great deal of money to the poor, which was a very nice gesture. No doubt he remembered from the old days how miserable it was not to have even a *skilling*. He was now rich and wore fine clothes, and had so many friends who all said that he was a pleasant fellow, a real gentleman, and that certainly pleased the soldier. But since he was spending money each day and not taking any in, he finally had no more than two *skillings* left and had to move out of the beautiful rooms where he had been living and into a tiny little garret room right under the roof. He had to brush his own boots and mend them with a darning needle, and none of his friends came to see him because there were too many stairs to climb.

It was a very dark evening, and he couldn't even afford to buy a candle, but then he remembered there was a little stump of one in the tinderbox he had taken from the hollow tree when the witch had helped him inside. He took out the tinderbox and the candle stump, but the minute he struck fire and sparks leaped from the flint, the door flew open and the dog that he had seen inside the tree, the one with eyes as big as two teacups, stood before him and said, 'What is my master's command?'

'What's this?' said the soldier. 'What an amusing

tinderbox, if I can wish for whatever I want! Bring me some money,' he said to the dog, and zip, he was gone; zip, he was back, holding a big sack of *skillings* in his mouth.

Now the soldier realized what a wonderful tinderbox it was. If he stuck it once, the dog who sat on the chest of copper coins came; if he struck it twice, the one with the silver coins came; and if he struck it three times, the one with the gold came. Now the soldier moved back downstairs to the beautiful rooms, dressed in fine clothing, and all his friends recognized him again, because they were so fond of him.

One day he thought, 'How odd that no one is allowed to see that princess. Everyone says she's supposed to be so lovely. But what good is it if she's always kept inside that enormous copper palace with all the towers? Couldn't I possibly have a look at her? Where's my tinderbox?' And then he struck fire and zip, the dog with eyes as big as teacups appeared.

'I know it's the middle of the night,' said the soldier, 'but I have such a great desire to see the princess, if only for a moment.'

The dog was out the door at once, and before the soldier knew it, he was back with the princess. She was sitting on the dog's back, asleep, and she was so lovely that anyone could see she was a real princess. The soldier couldn't resist, he had to kiss her, because he was a real soldier.

Then the dog ran back with the princess, but when morning came and the king and queen were pouring their tea, the princess said that she'd had a strange dream in the night about a dog and a soldier. She was riding on the dog's back, and the soldier had kissed her.

'That's certainly a fine story!' said the queen.

One of the old ladies-in-waiting was then ordered to keep watch at the bedside of the princess on the following night, to see if it was really a dream, or what else it might be.

The soldier was longing terribly to see the lovely princess once more, so the dog appeared in the night, picked her up, and ran as fast as he could, but the old lady-in-waiting put on her wading boots and ran just as swiftly right behind. When she saw them disappear inside a large building, she thought to herself: Now I know where it is. And with a piece of chalk she drew a big cross on the door. Then she returned home and went to bed, and the dog came back too, bringing the princess. But when he saw that a cross had been drawn on the door where the soldier lived, he took another piece of chalk and put a cross on all the doors in the whole city. That was a clever thing to do, because now the lady-in-waiting wouldn't be able to find the right door, since there were crosses on all of them.

Early the next morning the king and queen, the old lady-in-waiting, and all the officers went out to see where the princess had been.

'There it is!' said the king when he saw the first door with a cross on it.

'No, it's over there, my dear husband,' said the queen, who saw another door with a cross on it.

'But there's one there, and one there!' they all said. Wherever they looked, there was a cross on every door. Then they realized it was no use to go on searching.

But the queen was a very clever woman who was capable of more than just riding around in a coach. She took her big golden scissors, cut a large piece of silk into pieces, and then stitched together a charming little pouch, which she filled with fine grains of buckwheat. She tied it to the back of the princess, and when that was done, she cut a tiny hole in the pouch so the grains would sprinkle out wherever the princess went.

That night the dog appeared once again, put the princess on his back, and ran off with her to the soldier, who loved her so much and wanted dearly to be a prince so that he could make her his wife.

The dog didn't notice the grain sprinkling out all the way from the palace to the soldier's window, as he ran along the wall, carrying the princess. In the morning the king and queen could see quite well where their daughter had been, and they seized the soldier and threw him into jail.

And there he sat. Oh, how dark and dreary it was, and then they told him, 'Tomorrow you will hang.' That was not a pleasant thing to hear, and he had left his tinderbox behind at the inn. In the morning he could see through the iron bars on the little window that people were hurrying to the outskirts of the city to watch him hang. He heard the drums and saw the marching soldiers. Everyone was in a great rush, including a shoemaker's apprentice wearing a leather apron and slippers. He was moving along at such a gallop that one of his slippers flew off and struck the wall right where the soldier was sitting, peering out through the iron bars.

'Hey, shoemaker's apprentice! You don't have to be in such a rush,' said the soldier. 'Nothing's going to happen until I get there. But if you run over to the place where I was staying and bring me my tinderbox, I'll give you four *skill-ings*. But you have to be quick about it!' The shoemaker's apprentice wanted those four *skillings*, so he raced off to get the tinderbox, brought it to the soldier, and . . . well, let's hear what happened.

Outside the city a huge gallows had been built, and around it stood the soldiers and many hundreds of thousands of people. The king and queen sat on a lovely throne right across from the judge and the entire council.

The soldier was already standing on the ladder, but as they were about to put the rope around his neck, he said that before a sinner faced his punishment he was always allowed one harmless request. He dearly wanted to smoke a pipe of tobacco; it would be the last pipe he had in this world.

Now, that was not something the king could refuse, and so the soldier took out his tinderbox and struck fire, one, two, three! And there stood all three dogs: the one with eyes as big as teacups, the one with eyes like mill wheels, and the one with eyes as big as the Round Tower.

'Help me now, so I won't be hanged!' said the soldier, and then the dogs rushed at the judge and the entire council, seizing one by the leg and one by the nose, and flinging them high into the air so they fell back down and were crushed to bits.

'Not me!' said the king, but the biggest dog seized both him and the queen and tossed them after all the others. Then the soldiers were afraid, and all the people shouted, 'Little soldier, you shall be our king and wed the lovely princess!'

They put the soldier in the king's coach, and all three dogs danced before it, shouting, 'Hurrah!' The boys whistled through their fingers, and the soldiers presented arms. The princess came out of the copper palace and became queen, and that certainly pleased her! The wedding celebration lasted for a week, and the dogs sat at the table too, making big eyes.

Little Claus and Big Claus

There was a town where two men had the very same name. Both of them were named Claus, but one owned four horses while the other had only one. In order to tell them apart, people called the man with four horses Big Claus, and the man with only one horse Little Claus. Now we're going to hear what happened between those two, because this is a real story!

All week long Little Claus had to do the plowing for Big Claus, lending him his only horse. Then Big Claus would help him in return with all four of his horses, but only once a week, and that was on Sunday. Hee-ya! How Little Claus would crack his whip at all five horses. They might as well have belonged to him on that one day. The sun shone so wondrously, and all the bells in the tower rang, summoning people to church. Everyone was dressed in their best, walking with their hymnals under their arms, on their way to hear the pastor preach. And they looked at Little Claus, who was plowing with five horses, and he was so pleased that he cracked his whip again and shouted, 'Giddy-up, all my horses!'

'You shouldn't say that,' said Big Claus. 'Only one of those horses is yours.'

But when someone else passed by on his way to church,

Little Claus forgot that he wasn't supposed to say that and he shouted, 'Giddy-up, all my horses!'

'All right, now I really must ask you to stop that,' said Big Claus. 'Because if you say it one more time, I'm going to strike your horse on the forehead, and he'll drop dead on the spot, and that will be the end of him.'

'Well, I certainly won't say it again,' said Little Claus, but when people came past and nodded hello, he was so pleased and thought it looked so splendid that he had five horses plowing his field that he cracked his whip and shouted, 'Giddy-up, all my horses!'

'I'll giddy-up your horses!' said Big Claus, and he seized the tethering mallet and struck Little Claus's only horse on the forehead so that it fell to the ground, stone dead.

'Oh no, now I have no horse at all!' said Little Claus and began to cry. Later he flayed the horse and let the hide dry in the wind. Then he stuffed it in a sack that he hoisted onto his back and set off for town to sell his horsehide.

He had such a long way to go. He had to pass through a big, dark forest, and a terrible storm came up. He completely lost his way, and before he found the right road, dusk had fallen, and it was much too far to reach town or to go back home before night came.

Close to the road stood a large farm. The shutters on all the windows were closed, and yet there was a glimpse of light above. Surely they'll let me spend the night here, thought Little Claus, and he went over and knocked.

The farmer's wife opened the door, but when she heard what he wanted, she told him to keep on going. Her husband wasn't home, and she didn't take in strangers.

'Well, then I guess I'll have to sleep outside,' said Little Claus, and the farmer's wife shut the door in his face.

Nearby stood a big haystack, and between the haystack and house a little shed had been built with a flat, thatched roof.

'I can sleep up there,' said Little Claus when he saw the roof. 'That would make a lovely bed, and I'm sure the stork isn't going to fly down and bite me on the leg.' A real live stork was standing on the roof, where it had made a nest.

So Little Claus climbed up onto the shed, lay down, and turned onto his side to settle in properly. The wooden shutters on the windows of the house didn't quite meet at the top, which meant that he could peek into the room.

A great feast had been laid out with wine and a roast and such a lovely fish. The farmer's wife and the deacon were sitting at the table, all alone. She was pouring wine for him, and he began with the fish, because he was awfully fond of fish.

'If only I could have a bite too,' said Little Claus, craning his neck toward the window. Lord, what a lovely cake he could see in there. Oh yes, it was quite a feast.

Then he heard someone come riding along the road toward the house. It was the woman's husband, on his way home.

Now, it's true that he was a good man, but he had a strange affliction: He couldn't stand to see deacons. If he caught sight of a deacon, he would grow quite furious. That was also why the deacon had come to visit the woman when he knew that her husband wasn't home, and that's why the good woman had set out for him the best food she could offer. When they heard her husband coming, they were both terrified. The woman told the deacon to climb into a big empty chest that stood in the corner, which he did, because he knew full well that the poor man couldn't stand the sight of a deacon. The woman quickly hid all the wonderful food and wine inside her baking oven, because if her husband saw it, he was sure to ask what was going on.

'Oh no!' sighed Little Claus up on the shed when he saw all the food disappear.

'Is somebody up there?' asked the farmer, peering up at Little Claus. 'Why are you lying up there? Come on into the house!'

Then Little Claus told him how he had lost his way and asked if he might stay the night.

'Yes, of course,' said the farmer. 'But first we'll have a bite to eat.'

The woman welcomed them both, set dishes on a long table, and brought them a big bowl of porridge. The farmer was hungry and ate with gusto, but Little Claus couldn't help thinking about the wonderful roast, fish, and cake that he knew were hidden in the oven.

Under the table at his feet he had put the sack with the horsehide in it, because we know, after all, that this was what he had brought from home to sell in town. The porridge was not at all to his liking, and so he stepped on his sack, and the dry horsehide inside creaked quite loudly.

'Hush!' said Little Claus to his sack, but at the same instant he stepped on it again, and it creaked even louder than before.

'Tell me, what do you have in your bag?' asked the farmer.

'Oh, it's a troll,' said Little Claus. 'He says we shouldn't eat the porridge because he has conjured a whole oven full of roast and fish and cake.'

'Is that right?' said the farmer and quickly opened the oven. There he saw all the wonderful food that his wife had hidden, but he now thought the troll in the bag had conjured it up. His wife didn't dare say a word but set the food on the table at once, and so they ate the fish and the roast and the cake. Then Little Claus stepped on his sack again, making the hide creak.

'What's he saying now?' asked the farmer.

'He says,' said Little Claus, 'that he has also conjured up three bottles of wine for us, and they're standing over in the corner by the oven.' Then the woman had to bring out the wine she had hidden, and the farmer drank and grew quite merry. A troll like the one that Little Claus had in his bag was something that he would certainly like to own.

'Can he also conjure up the Devil?' asked the farmer. 'That's someone I'd really like to see, now that I'm feeling so merry.'

'Yes,' said Little Claus, 'my troll can do anything I ask. Isn't that right?' he said as he stepped on the bag, making it creak. 'Did you hear him say yes? But the Devil looks so horrid that you wouldn't want to look at him.'

'Oh, I'm not the least bit afraid. How bad do you think he could look?'

'Well, he's going to look exactly like a deacon.'

'Whoa!' said the farmer. 'That's ghastly, all right. I must tell you that I can't stand the sight of deacons. But that doesn't matter, because I'll know it's the Devil, so it won't bother me as much. I'm feeling brave now. But don't let him come too close.'

'Let me ask my troll,' said Little Claus, and he stepped on the bag, cupping his ear.

'What does he say?'

'He says that you can go over and open the chest that's standing in the corner, and you'll see the Devil moping inside, but you have to hold on to the lid so he doesn't get out.'

'Come and help me hold on to it,' said the farmer, and he went over to the chest where his wife had hidden the real deacon, who sat there completely terrified.

The farmer lifted the lid slightly and peeked inside. 'Whoa!' he yelled, jumping back. 'I saw him all right, and he looks just like our deacon! Oh, that was terrible!'

After that they had to have a drink, and then they kept on drinking until late into the night.

'You've got to sell me that troll,' said the farmer. 'Ask whatever price you like. Why, I'd even give you a whole bushelful of money!'

'No, I can't do that,' that Claus. 'Just think how much I'll gain from owning this troll.'

'Oh, but I'd certainly like to have it,' said the farmer, and he kept on begging.

'All right,' said Little Claus at last. 'Since you've been kind enough to give me shelter for the night, I can't refuse. You can have the troll for a bushel of money, but I want the bushel to be full to the brim.'

'And that's what you'll get,' said the farmer, 'but you have to take that chest over there with you. I refuse to have it in the house for even an hour longer. There's no telling whether he's still inside.'

Little Claus gave the farmer the sack with the dried horse-hide and got in return a whole bushel of money, full to the brim. The farmer even presented him with a big wheelbarrow for carrying the money and the chest.

'Farewell!' said Little Claus, and then he set off with his money and the big chest in which the deacon was still sitting.

On the other side of the woods was a big, deep river. The water was running so fast that it was almost impossible to swim against the current. A big new bridge had been built across it. Little Claus stopped in the middle of the bridge and said very loudly so that the deacon inside the chest would hear him:

'Well, what do I need this stupid chest for? It's so heavy it feels like it's full of rocks. I'm getting awfully tired of carting it around, so I think I'll throw it in the river. If it floats home to me, that's fine, but if it doesn't, it won't matter at all.'

Then he grabbed one handle of the chest and lifted it slightly, as if he were going to shove it into the water.

'No, stop!' yelled the deacon inside the chest. 'Let me out!'

'Ooh!' said Little Claus, pretending to be scared. 'He's still inside! I've got to toss it in the river as quick as I can so he'll drown.'

'Oh no, oh no!' shouted the deacon. 'I'll give you a whole bushelful of money if you don't.'

'Well, that's a different story,' said Little Claus, and opened the chest. The deacon crawled out at once, shoved the empty chest into the water, and went off to his house, where he gave

Little Claus a whole bushelful of money. Little Claus already had one bushel from the farmer; now his whole wheelbarrow was full of money.

'Look at that, I certainly did get a good price for that horse,' he said to himself when he came back to his own house and dumped all the money in a big heap in the middle of the floor. 'Big Claus will be annoyed when he finds out how rich I've become from my only horse, but I'm not going to come right out and tell him about it.'

Then he sent a boy over to Big Claus to borrow a bushel measure.

'I wonder what he wants it for,' thought Big Claus, and smeared tar inside the bottom so that a little of whatever was being weighed would stick to it. And it did, because when he got the bushel measure back, there were three new silver eight-*skilling* coins stuck to it.

'What's this?' said Big Claus and ran right over to see Little Claus. 'Where did you get all this money?'

'Oh, I got it for my horsehide. I sold it last night.'

'That was certainly a good price!' said Big Claus, and he raced back home, picked up an ax, and struck every one of his four horses on the forehead. Then he skinned them and drove into town with the hides.

'Hides! Hides! Who wants to buy hides?' he shouted through the streets.

All the shoemakers and tanners came running and asked him how much he wanted for the hides.

'A bushel of money for each of them,' said Big Claus.

'Are you crazy?' they all said. 'Do you think we have bushels of money?'

'Hides, hides! Who wants to buy hides?' he shouted again, but to everyone who asked how much the hides cost, he replied, 'A bushel of money.'

'He's trying to make fools of us,' they all said. Then the shoemakers picked up their straps and the tanners their leather aprons, and they all started beating Big Claus.

'Hides, hides!' they jeered at him. 'Oh yes, we'll give you a hide that bleeds like a pig! Now get out of town!' they shouted, and Big Claus had to rush off as fast as he could. He had never been beaten so badly in his life.

'Well!' he said when he got home. 'Little Claus is going to pay for this. I'm going to murder him for this!'

But back at Little Claus's house his grandmother had just died. Now, it's true that she had been terribly ill-tempered and mean toward him, but even so he was quite sad. He took the dead woman and put her in his warm bed to see whether she might come back to life. There she would lie all night long while he slept in the corner, sitting on a chair; that was something he had done before.

As he was sitting there that night, the door opened and Big Claus came in with an ax. He knew where Little Claus's bed stood, and he went right over a struck the dead grandmother on the forehead, thinking that it was Little Claus.

'Take that!' he said. 'Now you won't make a fool of me anymore.' And then he went back home.

'What a mean and evil man,' said Little Claus. 'He wanted to murder me, but it's a good thing the old lady was already dead, or he would have taken her life.'

Then he dressed his old grandmother in her Sunday best, borrowed a horse from his neighbor, harnessed it to his wagon, and put his old grandmother on the back seat so that she wouldn't fall out when he started driving. Then they headed off through the woods. When the sun came up, they were outside a big inn, where Little Claus stopped and went inside to get a bite to eat.

The innkeeper was very, very rich, and he was also a good man, but hot-tempered, as if there were pepper and tobacco inside of him.

'Good morning,' he said to Little Claus. 'You've put on your fine clothes awfully early today.'

'Yes,' said Little Claus, 'I'm going to town with my old grandmother. She's sitting outside in the wagon, and I can't get her to come indoors. Would you mind taking her a glass of mead? But you'll have to speak up because she doesn't hear very well.'

'Why, certainly,' said the innkeeper. He poured a big glass of mead and took it outside to the dead grandmother, who was propped up in the wagon.

'Here's a glass of mead from your grandson,' said the innkeeper, but the dead woman didn't say a word, just sat there without moving.

'Didn't you hear me?' shouted the innkeeper as loud as he could. 'Here's a glass of mead from your grandson!'

Once again he shouted the same thing, and then one more time, but when she didn't budge in the slightest, he got angry and tossed the glass of mead right in her face so it ran down her nose. And she toppled over backward into the wagon, because she had merely been propped up but wasn't tied down.

'What's this?' shouted Little Claus as he came running out the door and grabbed the innkeeper by the shirtfront. 'You've gone and killed my grandmother! Just look at that big hole in her forehead!'

'Oh, what bad luck!' cried the innkeeper, wringing his hands. 'It's all the fault of my bad temper. Dear Little Claus, I'll give you a whole bushelful of money and pay for your grandmother's burial as if she were my own, but don't say a word or they'll chop off my head, and that would be awful!'

So Little Claus got a whole bushelful of money, and the innkeeper buried the old grandmother as if she were his own.

As soon as Little Claus got back home with all the money, he at once sent his boy over to see Big Claus, to ask if he could borrow a bushel measure.

'What's this?' said Big Claus. 'I thought I killed him! I'm going to have to see this for myself.' And so he took the bushel measure over to Little Claus in person.

'Where on earth did you get all that money?' he asked, opening his eyes wide when he saw how much more Little Claus had accumulated.

'It was my grandmother, not me that you killed,' said Little Claus. 'But now I've sold her for a bushelful of money.'

'That was certainly a good price,' said Big Claus, and he rushed home, picked up an ax, and promptly killed his old grandmother. He put her in his wagon, drove into town to the apothecary's shop, and asked him whether he wanted to buy a dead body.

'Who is it, and where did you get it?' asked the apothecary.

'It's my grandmother,' said Big Claus. 'I've killed her for a bushelful of money.'

'Good Lord!' said the apothecary. 'You don't know what you're saying! Don't say things like that or you could lose your head.' And then he told him exactly what a dreadful, evil thing he had done, and what a bad person he was, and that he ought to be punished. Big Claus was so scared that he leaped straight from the apothecary's shop into his wagon, cracked his whip at the horses, and raced off home. The apothecary and everyone else thought he was mad, and so they let him go where he liked.

'You're going to pay for this!' said Big Claus when he was out on the road. 'Oh yes, you're going to pay for this, Little Claus!' As soon as he got home he took the biggest sack he could find and went over to Little Claus and said, 'You've made a fool of me again. First I killed my horses, and then my old grandmother. It's all your fault, but you're never going to trick me again.' And he grabbed Little Claus around the waist and stuffed him into the sack. Then he slung him over his back and shouted, 'Now I'm going to take you out and drown you!'

It was a long walk to reach the river, and Little Claus wasn't easy to carry. The road passed very close to the church, where the organ was playing and people were singing so beautifully inside. Then Big Claus put down the sack holding Little Claus right next to the church door, thinking that it might do him good to go inside and listen to a hymn first, before continuing on his way. Little Claus couldn't get out, and everyone else was in church, so Big Claus went inside.

'Oh me, oh my!' sighted Little Claus from inside the sack. He twisted and turned, but it was impossible for him to loosen the cord. At that moment an old, old cattle-driver with chalk-white hair and a big walking stick in his hand came by. He was driving a big herd of cows and bulls in front of him. They trampled over the sack that Claus was in, tumbling it onto its side.

'Oh my,' sighed Little Claus. 'I'm so young, but I'm already headed for Heaven.'

'And what a poor man am I,' said the cattle-driver. 'Here I am so old but it's not yet my time to go.'

'Open the sack!' shouted Little Claus. 'Climb in and take my place, and you'll end up in Heaven at once.'

'Oh, I'd like that very much,' said the cattle-driver, untying the sack. And Little Claus jumped right out.

'Could you take care of the cattle?' said the old man, and he climbed into the bag, which Little Claus tied up and then went on his way, taking along the cows and bulls.

A little while later Big Claus came out of the church and hoisted the sack onto his back, thinking that it certainly was a lot lighter, because the old cattle-driver was no more than half the weight of Little Claus. 'How easy it is to carry him now! Well, that's probably because I've been listening to a hymn.' Then he went over to the river, which was deep and wide, threw the sack with the old cattle-driver into the water, and shouted after him, thinking he was Little Claus, 'Take that! Now you won't be making a fool of me anymore!'

Then he headed home, but when he came to the crossroads, he met Little Claus walking along with all his cattle.

'What's this?' said Big Claus. 'Didn't I drown you?'

'Yes, you did,' said Little Claus. 'You threw me in the river less than half an hour ago.'

'But where did you get all these wonderful cattle?' asked Big Claus.

'They're sea cattle,' said Little Claus. 'Let me tell you the whole story. And by the way, thanks for drowning me, because now I'm back on my feet and let me tell you, I'm as rich as can be! I was so scared when I was inside that sack, and the wind whistled in my ears when you threw me off the bridge and into the cold water. I sank straight to the bottom, but I didn't hurt myself because the loveliest soft grass grows down there. That's where I landed, and the bag was opened at once. The loveliest maiden, wearing chalk-white clothing and with a green wreath on her wet hair, took my hand and said, "Is that you, Little Claus? Well, first let me give you these cattle. Five miles up the road there's another whole herd that I want you to have." Then I saw that the river was a great highway for the sea folk. Down on the bottom they were walking and driving all the way from the sea toward land, to the place where the river ends. It was so lovely with flowers and the freshest of grass, and fish swimming in the water; they flitted around my ears like the birds in the air. How handsome the people were and how many cattle there were, ambling along the ditches and fences.'

'But why did you come back to us so soon?' asked Big Claus. 'That's not what I would have done if it was so charming down there.'

'Well, you see,' said Little Claus, 'it was really very cunning of me. You heard me say that the mermaid told me that five miles up the road – and by road she meant the river, of course, since she can't travel any other way – there was a whole herd of cattle waiting for me. I happen to know where the river starts to bend, first one way and then the other, making a whole detour. It's much shorter, if you can do it, to come up here on land and head straight across to the river. That way I saved almost two and a half miles and reached my sea cattle much quicker.'

'Oh, you certainly are a lucky man!' said Big Claus. 'Do you think I could get some sea cattle too, if I went down to the bottom of the river?'

'Oh yes, I imagine so,' said Little Claus. 'But I can't carry you in a sack to the river; you're much too heavy for me. But if you walk there yourself and then climb into the bag, I'd be more than happy to throw you in.'

'Thanks so much,' said Big Claus. 'But if I don't get any sea cattle when I get there, I'm going to give you a beating, believe you me!'

'Oh no! Don't be so mean!' And then they went down to the river. The cattle were so thirsty that when they saw the water, they ran as fast as they could down the slope to drink.

'Look how fast they're moving,' said Little Claus. 'They're longing to go back down to the bottom.'

'Yes, but help me first,' said Big Claus. 'Otherwise I'll give you a beating!' And then he climbed into the big sack that was lying across the back of one of the bulls. 'Put a rock inside, because otherwise I'm afraid I won't sink,' said Big Claus.

'Oh, I'm sure you will,' said Little Claus, but just the same, he put a big rock in the sack, tied the cord tight, and then gave it a shove. Plop! Big Claus landed in the river and promptly sank to the bottom.

'I'm afraid he's not going to find any cattle,' said Little Claus, and then he headed home with all he had.

The Princess on the Pea

Once upon a time there was a prince. He wanted a princess, but she had to be a real princess. So he traveled all over the world to find one, but wherever he went there was something wrong. There were plenty of princesses, but he wasn't quite sure if they were real princesses. There was always something that wasn't quite right. Then he went back home and was so sad because he dearly wanted to have a real princess.

One evening there was a terrible storm. Lightning flashed and thunder roared, the rain poured down, it was simply dreadful! Then there was a knock at the town gate, and the old king went to open it.

There was a princess standing outside. But good Lord how she looked because of the rain and terrible weather! Water was streaming from her hair and her clothes, running in the toes of her shoes and out of the heels. Then she said that she was a real princess.

'Well, we'll see about that,' thought the old queen, but she didn't say a word. She went into the bedroom, took off all the bedclothes, and placed a pea at the bottom of the bed. Then she took twenty mattresses and put them on top of the pea, and another twenty eiderdown quilts on top of the mattresses.

That's where the princess was to sleep that night.

The next morning they asked her how she had slept.

'Oh, dreadfully!' said the princess. 'I hardly closed my eyes all night. Lord knows what there was in my bed. I was lying on something hard, and I'm black and blue all over! It's simply dreadful!'

Then they could see that she was a real princess, since she had felt the pea through those twenty mattresses and those twenty eiderdown quilts. No one else could have such tender skin except for a real princess.

And so the prince took her as his wife, because now he knew that he had a real princess. And the pea was placed in the Royal Curiosity Cabinet, where it can still be seen today, as long as no one has taken it.

Now you see, that was a real story!

The Steadfast Tin Soldier

Once upon a time there were twenty-five tin soldiers. They were brothers, because they were all born from an old tin spoon. Rifles they held at their shoulders, and their faces looked straight ahead. Red and blue, and oh so lovely were their uniforms. When the lid was removed from the box in which they lay, the very first words they heard in the world were, 'Tin soldiers!' That's what a little boy cried, clapping his hands. They had been given to him because it was his birthday, and now he lined them up on the table. Each soldier looked exactly like the next, except for one who was slightly different. He had only one leg because he was the last to be cast, and there wasn't enough tin left. Yet he stood just as firmly on one leg as the others did on two, and he's the one who turned out to be remarkable.

On the table where they stood were many other toys, but the one that was most striking was a charming castle made of paper. Through the tiny windows you could see right into the halls. Outside stood small trees around a little mirror that was meant to look like a lake. Swans made of wax were swimming around on it, reflected in the mirror. The whole thing was so charming, and yet the most charming of all was a little maiden who stood in the open doorway to the castle. She had also been cut out of paper, but she was wearing a skirt of the sheerest tulle and a tiny narrow blue ribbon over her shoulder like a sash. In the middle sat a gleaming spangle as big as her face. The little maiden was stretching out both arms, because she was a dancer, and she was also lifting one leg so high in the air that the tin soldier couldn't see it at all, and he thought that she had only one leg, just like him.

'Now there's a wife for me!' he thought. 'But she looks rather refined, and she lives in a castle. I have only a box, and it has to hold twenty-five of us. That's no place for her! Still, I have to see about making her acquaintance.' And then he stretched out full-length behind a snuff box that stood on the table. From there he could get a good look at the elegant little lady, who continued to stand on one leg without losing her balance.

Later that evening all the other tin soldiers were put back in their box, and the people of the house went to bed. Then the toys began to play. They gave tea parties, fought battles, and danced. The tin soldiers rattled in their box because they wanted to play too, but they couldn't open the lid. The nutcracker turned somersaults, and the slate pencil scribbled all over the slate. There was such a commotion that the canary woke up and started chattering too, and in verse, of all things. The only two who didn't budge were the tin soldier and the little dancer. She held herself erect on her toes, with her arms held out. He was just as steadfast on one leg, and his eyes didn't leave her for a second.

Then the clock struck twelve, and *Bam!* the lid of the snuff box flew open, but there was no tobacco inside – no, there was a little black troll. What a wily trick that was.

'Tin soldier!' said the troll. 'Keep your eyes to yourself!'

But the tin soldier pretended not to hear him.

'Well, just wait till morning,' said the troll.

When morning came and the children got up, the tin soldier was moved over to the windowsill, and whether it was the troll or a gust of wind, all of a sudden the window flew open and the soldier plummeted headfirst from the fourth floor. What a terrifying speed, with his leg turned upward! He landed on his cap, with his bayonet stuck between the cobblestones.

The servant girl and the little boy went downstairs at once to look for him, but even though they nearly stepped on him, they couldn't see him. If the tin soldier had shouted 'Here I am!' they probably would have found him, but he didn't think it was proper to yell when he was in uniform.

Then it started to rain. One drop came down faster than the other; it turned into a regular downpour. When it was over, two street urchins came along.

'Hey, look!' said one of them. 'There's a tin soldier lying here. Let's send him out for a sail.'

And so they made a boat out of newspaper, set the tin soldier in the middle of it, and he sailed off down the gutter. The two boys ran alongside, clapping their hands. God save us, what waves there were in that gutter, and what a current! Well, it's true that there had just been a downpour. The paper boat pitched up and down, and at times it would spin so fast that the tin soldier swayed. But he remained steadfast, his expression unflinching, standing erect with his rifle at his shoulder.

All of a sudden the boat washed in under a plank that lay over the gutter. It grew just as dark as inside his box.

'I wonder where I'll end up now,' he thought. 'Yes, well,

this is all the troll's fault. Oh, if only the little maiden were sitting here in the boat, then I wouldn't care if it was twice as dark!'

At that moment a big water rat appeared. It lived under the gutter plank.

'Have you got a travel pass?' asked the rat. 'Let's see your travel pass!'

But the tin soldier didn't say a word, holding his rifle even tighter. The boat raced along, with the rat right behind. Oh, how it gnashed its teeth, shouting to sticks and pieces of straw:

'Stop him! Stop him! He didn't pay the toll! He didn't show his travel pass!'

But the current grew stronger and stronger. The tin soldier could already glimpse daylight up ahead where the plank ended, but he also heard a roaring sound that would scare even a brave man. Just imagine: Where the plank ended, the gutter plunged right into a huge canal. For him it would be just as dangerous as for us to sail over an enormous waterfall.

He was already so close that he couldn't stop. The boat rushed forward; the poor tin soldier held himself as upright as he could. No one was going to say that he so much as blinked an eye. The boat spun around three or four times and filled with water up to the rim. It was going to sink. The tin soldier was standing in water up to his neck, and the boat sank deeper and deeper, the paper began dissolving faster and faster. Then the water was over the soldier's head. That's when he thought about the charming little dancer, whom he would never see again. And in his ears the soldier heard:

'Flee, warrior, flee!
Death is after you!'

Then the paper fell apart, and the tin soldier plunged right through. But at that very instant he was swallowed by a big fish.

Oh, how dark it was inside! It was even worse than under the gutter plank, and it was much more cramped. But the tin soldier was steadfast and stretched out full-length with his rifle at his shoulder.

The fish thrashed about, making the most terrifying movements. Finally it grew quite still, and what looked like a bolt of lightning flashed through it. The light shone so bright, and someone cried loudly, 'Tin soldier!' The fish had been caught, brought to market, sold, and then ended up in a kitchen where the servant girl slit it open with a big knife. Putting two fingers around his waist, she plucked out the soldier and carried him into the parlor where everyone wanted to see the remarkable man who had traveled inside the belly of a fish. But the tin soldier was not the least bit proud of himself. They set him on the table and there . . . Oh, what strange things can happen in the world! The tin soldier was in the very same parlor where he had been before. He saw the very same children and the toys on the table and the lovely castle with the charming little dancer. She was still standing on one leg with the other lifted high in the air. She too was steadfast. The tin soldier was touched, he was just about to weep tears of tin, but that wouldn't be proper. He looked at her and she looked at him, but neither said a word.

At that moment one of the little boys picked up the soldier and tossed him right into the stove, giving no explanation at all. The troll in the box was most certainly to blame.

The tin soldier stood there, brightly lit, and felt a terrible heat, but whether it was from the actual fire or from love, he didn't know. The paint had worn right off him, but whether this had happened on his journey or from sorrow, no one could say. He looked at the little maiden, she looked at him, and he felt himself melting. But he still stood there, steadfast, with his rifle at his shoulder. Then a door opened, the wind seized hold of the dancer, and she flew like a sylph right into the stove to the tin soldier, burst into flame, and was gone. Then the tin soldier melted into a lump, and the next day, when the servant girl took out the ashes, she found him in the shape of a little tin heart. But all that was left of the dancer was the spangle, and that had been burned black as coal.

The Nightingale

In China, as you probably know, the Emperor is Chinese, and everyone around him is Chinese too. This story happened many years ago, but that's precisely why it's worth hearing, before it's forgotten. The Emperor's palace was the most magnificent in the world, made entirely of fine porcelain, so costly but so fragile, so delicate to the touch that you had to be extremely careful. In the garden you could see the most wondrous flowers. Tied to the most splendid of them were silver bells that jingled, and you couldn't walk past without noticing the flowers. Yes, everything was quite artful in the Emperor's garden, which stretched so far that even the gardener didn't know where it ended. If you kept on walking you would come to the loveliest forest with tall trees and deep lakes. The forest went right down to the sea, which was deep and blue. Great ships could sail right under the branches. And among the branches lived a nightingale who sang so blissfully that even the poor fisherman, who had many other things to tend to, would lie still and listen whenever he heard the nightingale as he pulled in his fishing nets at night. 'Dear Lord, how beautiful she sounds!' he said.

But then he had to go back to his work and forget about the bird. Yet the next night when she sang again and the fisherman appeared, he would say the same thing, 'Dear Lord, how beautiful she sounds!'

Travelers came from countries all over the world to admire the Emperor's city and the palace and the garden. But if they happened to hear the nightingale, they all said, 'That's the best thing of all!'

The travelers would talk about everything when they went back home, and the learned men wrote many books about the city, the palace, and the garden, but they didn't forget the nightingale; she was esteemed above all else. Those who could write poetry wrote the loveliest poems, every single one about the nightingale in the forest by the deep sea.

These books circulated around the world, and one day some of them even reached the Emperor. He sat on his golden chair, reading and reading, as he kept nodding his head, because it pleased him to hear the magnificent descriptions of the city, the palace, and the garden. 'Yet the nightingale is the best of all!' he read in the book.

'What's this?' said the Emperor. 'The nightingale? I know nothing about it! Is there such a bird in my empire, let alone in my own garden? I've never heard of her. To think I had to learn about her from a book!'

And then he called for his Lord Chamberlain, who was so refined that if anyone lower in rank dared speak to him or ask him about something, his only reply was 'P!' And that means nothing at all.

'Supposedly there is a truly extraordinary bird here called the nightingale,' said the Emperor. 'They say that she's the best thing in all my vast domain. Why hasn't anyone told me about her?'

'I've never heard her mentioned before,' said the Lord Chamberlain. 'She has never been presented at court.'

'I want her to come here tonight and sing for me,' said the Emperor. 'The whole world knows what I have, but I do not.'

'I've never heard her mentioned before,' said the Lord Chamberlain. 'I'll search for her, I'll find her!'

But where was she to be found? The Lord Chamberlain ran up and down all the stairs, through the halls and corridors. Not a single person he met had ever heard mention of the nightingale. So the Lord Chamberlain ran back to the Emperor and said that she must be a fable concocted by those who write books. 'Your Imperial Majesty should not believe what people write. It's all fabrication and what's called black magic.'

'But the book I was reading was sent to me by the mighty Emperor of Japan,' said the Emperor, 'so it must be true. I want to hear the nightingale. She must be here tonight! I bestow on her my highest favor! And if she doesn't come, then all the members of the court will be punched in the stomach after they've eaten their supper.'

'*Xing-pei!*' said the Lord Chamberlain, and once again he ran up and down all the stairs, through all the halls and corridors. And half the court ran along with him, because they didn't want to be punched in the stomach. Everyone was asking about the remarkable nightingale that was known to the whole world but to no one at court.

Finally they came upon a poor little girl in the kitchen, and she said, 'Oh Lord, the nightingale! I know her well. Yes, how she can sing! Every evening I'm allowed to take home a few scraps from the table for my poor sick mother. She lives down near the shore, and when I walk back feeling tired, I take a rest in the forest, and then I hear the nightingale singing. It makes my eyes fill with tears. It's as if my mother were kissing me.'

'Little kitchen maid,' said the Lord Chamberlain, 'I shall arrange a permanent post for you in the kitchen and permission to watch the Emperor eat if you can lead us to the nightingale. She has been summoned here tonight.'

And so they all set off for the forest, to the place where the nightingale usually sang. Half the court went along. As they were walking, a cow began to moo.

'Oh!' said the royal squires. 'Now we've found her. What remarkable power for such a small creature! We're quite certain we've heard her before.'

'No, those are the cows mooing,' said the little kitchen maid. 'We're still quite far from the place.'

Now the frogs began croaking in the bog.

'Lovely!' said the Chinese Court Chaplain. 'Now I can hear her. It sounds just like little church bells.'

'No, those are the frogs,' said the little kitchen maid. 'But I think we'll hear her soon.'

Then the nightingale began to sing.

'There she is,' said the little girl. 'Listen! Listen! And there she sits!' And then she pointed at a little gray bird up in the branches.

'Is it possible?' said the Lord Chamberlain. 'That's not at all how I imagined her. How plain she looks! She must have lost her color from seeing so many refined people all around.'

'Little nightingale!' cried the little kitchen maid in a loud voice. 'Our Most Gracious Emperor would like so much for you to sing for him.'

'With the greatest pleasure,' said the nightingale and sang so it was sheer delight.

'It sounds just like glass bells,' said the Lord Chamberlain. 'And look at her little throat – she's singing with all her might. It's strange that we've never heard this bird before. She will be a huge success at court.'

'Shall I sing some more for the Emperor?' asked the nightingale, who thought the Emperor was among them.

'My splendid little nightingale,' said the Lord Chamberlain, 'I have the great pleasure of summoning you to a royal celebration this evening, where you will enchant His Exalted Imperial Grace with your charming song.'

'My song sounds best out in nature,' said the nightingale, but she willingly went along with them when she heard that this was the Emperor's wish.

At the palace everything had been properly cleaned and polished. The walls and floors, which were made of porcelain, gleamed with thousands of golden lamps. The loveliest flowers, the ones with bells attached, had been placed in the corridors; there was a draft and a great commotion, making all the bells ring. You couldn't hear yourself think.

In the middle of the great hall, where the Emperor was seated, a golden perch had been placed, and that was where the nightingale was to sit. The entire court was present, and the little kitchen maid had been given permission to stand behind the door, since she now held the title of Real Kitchen Maid. Everyone was dressed in his very finest, and everyone was looking at the little gray bird, to whom the Emperor nodded.

And the nightingale sang so wondrously that tears filled the Emperor's eyes. Tears rolled down his cheeks, and then the nightingale sang even more beautifully; the song went straight to the heart. The Emperor was so happy that he said the nightingale must wear his golden slipper around her neck. But the nightingale thanked him and said that she had already received reward enough.

'I've seen tears in the Emperor's eyes. For me that is the richest treasure. An emperor's tears have a wondrous power. God knows, that is reward enough.' And then she sang again in her sweet, blessed voice.

'This is the most lovable coquetry we've ever known,' said the women all around, and then they put water in their mouths in order to cluck whenever anyone spoke to them. They thought they too could be nightingales. Even the lackeys and chambermaids announced that they were satisfied, and that is saying a great deal because they're the most difficult of all to please. Yes, the nightingale certainly was a success!

Now she would stay at court, and have her own cage, as well as the freedom to promenade twice a day and once at night. Twelve servants were sent along, each of them holding tight to a silk ribbon attached to her leg. There wasn't the least bit of pleasure in those excursions.

The whole city was talking about the extraordinary bird. If two people met, one of them would say to the other 'Night!' and the other would say 'Gale!' and then they would sigh, fully understanding each other. Why, eleven grocers' children were named after her, but not one of them could even carry a tune.

One day a big package arrived for the Emperor. On the outside it said: 'Nightingale.'

'Here we have a new book about our famous bird,' said the Emperor. But it wasn't a book. A little work of art lay inside the box, a mechanical nightingale that was supposed to look like the live one, although it was completely encrusted with diamonds, rubies, and sapphires. As soon as they wound up the mechanical bird it sang one of the tunes that the real bird sang, and its tail moved up and down, glittering with silver and gold. Around its neck hung a little ribbon, and on it were the words: 'The Emperor of Japan's nightingale is paltry compared to the Emperor of China's.'

'It's lovely!' they all said, and the person who had brought the mechanical bird was at once given the title of Supreme Imperial Nightingale Bringer.

'Let's have them sing together. What a duet that will be!'

And then they had to sing together, but it was not a success, because the real nightingale sang in her own way, while the mechanical bird ran on cylinders. 'There's nothing wrong with that,' said the Music Master. 'It keeps perfect time and is obviously a follower of my own methods.' Then the mechanical bird had to sing alone. It brought just as much joy as the real bird, and on top of that it was much more charming in appearance. It glittered like bracelets and brooches.

Thirty-three times it sang the very same tune, and yet it never grew tired. Everyone could have listened to it all over again, but the Emperor felt that the live nightingale should also sing a little. But where was she? No one had noticed that she had flown out the open window, off to her green forests.

41

'Well, what sort of behavior is that?' said the Emperor. And all the members of court began scolding, saying that the nightingale was a most ungrateful creature. 'Yet we have the best bird of all,' they said, and then the mechanical bird had to sing some more, and that was the thirty-fourth time they heard the same tune. But they didn't yet know it by heart, because it was so complicated, and the Music Master lavished great praise on the bird. Yes, he assured them that it was better than the real nightingale, not only in terms of its attire and the scores of lovely diamonds, but also internally.

'For you see, ladies and gentlemen, and above all Your Imperial Highness! You can never count on what will come out of the real nightingale, but with the mechanical bird everything is certain. This is how it will sound, and no other way. You can explain it, you can open it up and demonstrate the human reasoning, how the cylinders are arranged, how they operate, and how one turns the other.'

'Those are my thoughts exactly,' they all said. And the Music Master was granted permission, on the following Sunday, to display the bird to the people. They too should hear it sing, said the Emperor. And they heard it and were as pleased as if they had drunk themselves giddy on tea; that was so typically Chinese. And everyone said 'Oh!' and held up in the air the finger that we call 'pot-licker' and then they nodded. But the poor fishermen who had heard the real nightingale said, 'It sounds nice enough, and it does look quite like it, but something is missing, we don't know what.'

The real nightingale was banished from the realm.

The mechanical bird had its place on a silk pillow close to

the Emperor's bed. All the gifts it had been given, gold and precious stones, were spread around it, and in title it had risen to Supreme Imperial Nightstand Singer. In rank it was number one on the left, because the Emperor considered the side of the heart to be the most noble, and even in an Emperor the heart is on the left. The Music Master wrote twenty-five volumes about the mechanical bird, books that were so learned and so lengthy, and written in the most difficult of Chinese words, that everyone said they had read and understood them, because otherwise they would have seemed stupid and then they would have been punched in the stomach.

A whole year passed in this fashion. The Emperor, the court, and all the other Chinese people knew by heart every little cluck of the mechanical bird's song, but that was precisely why they liked it above all else. They could sing it themselves, and they did. The street urchins sang 'Xi-xi-xi! Cluck-cluck-cluck!' And the Emperor sang it too. Oh yes, it was certainly lovely!

But one evening when the mechanical bird was singing its best and the Emperor was lying in bed and listening, it went 'Clunk!' inside. Something burst. 'Buzzzzzz!' all the gears spun around, and then the music stopped.

The Emperor sprang out of bed at once and called for his royal physician, but what good could he do? Then they summoned the watchmaker. After much discussion and a great deal of study, he managed to get the bird working fairly well, but he said that it would have to be played sparingly because the cylinder pegs were worn out. It would be impossible to replace them with new ones so that the music would play properly. That was a terrible shame! Only once a year did they dare let the mechanical bird sang, and even that was almost too often. But then the Music Master gave a little speech using big words and said that it was just as good as new, and so it was just as good as new.

Five years passed, and the whole land suffered a great sadness, because everyone was truly very fond of their Emperor. Now they said he was ill and about to die. A new emperor had already been chosen, and the people stood outside on the street and asked the Lord Chamberlain how things were going with their Emperor.

'P!' he said and shook his head.

Cold and pale, the Emperor lay in his big, magnificent bed. The entire court thought he was dead, and all of them had run off to greet the new Emperor. The valets had run outside to talk about it, and the palace maids were holding a big coffee party. All around in the halls and corridors cloth had been laid down so that no one's footsteps could be heard. That's why it was so quiet, so quiet. But the Emperor was not yet dead. Rigid and pale, he lay in the magnificent bed with the long velvet curtains and the heavy gold tassels. High above, a window stood open, and the moon was shining on the Emperor and the mechanical bird.

The poor Emperor could hardly breathe; it felt as if something were sitting on his chest. He opened his eyes and saw that it was Death sitting on his chest. He had put on the gold crown and was holding in one hand the Emperor's gold sword, and in the other his magnificent banner. All around in the folds of the great velvet bed curtains peculiar heads were sticking out, some of them quite horrid, others so blessedly gentle. They were all of the Emperor's good and bad deeds, looking at him, now that Death was sitting on his heart.

'Do you remember this?' one after the other whispered. 'Do you remember this?' And then they told him so many things that the sweat poured from his brow.

'I never knew that!' said the Emperor. 'Music, music, the great Chinese drum!' he shouted. 'So I won't have to listen to everything they're saying.'

But they kept on, and Death nodded, as the Chinese do, at everything that was said.

'Music, music!' screamed the Emperor. 'You blessed little golden bird! Sing now, sing! I've given you gold and precious things. I myself have hung my golden slipper around your neck. So sing now, sing!'

But the bird stood silent. There was no one to wind it up, and otherwise it couldn't sing. But Death kept on looking at the Emperor with his big, empty eye sockets, and it was so quiet, so horribly quiet.

At that moment, close to the window, the loveliest song was heard. It was the live little nightingale, who was sitting on a branch outside. She had heard about the Emperor's distress, and that's why she had come, to offer solace and hope. And as she sang, the figures grew more and more pale, the blood began to flow faster and faster through the Emperor's weak limbs, and Death himself listened and said, 'Keep singing, little nightingale! Keep singing!'

'Yes, if you give me the magnificent gold sword! Yes, if you give me the opulent banner! If you give me the Emperor's crown!'

And Death returned each treasure for a song, and the nightingale still kept singing. She sang of the silent church-yard where the white roses grow, where the fragrant elder tree stands, and where the fresh grass is watered by the tears of the bereaved. Then Death had such a longing for his own garden that he floated out like a cold white fog, out the window.

'Thank you, thank you!' said the Emperor. 'You heavenly little bird, of course I recognize you! You're the one I chased from my realm. And yet you have sung the evil visions away from my bed and driven Death from my heart. How shall I reward you?'

'You have already rewarded me,' said the nightingale. 'I won tears from your eyes the first time I sang. I will never forget that about you. They are the jewels that make a sing-er's heart glad. But sleep now and grow strong and healthy. I will sing for you.'

And she sang. The Emperor fell into a sweet slumber, so gentle and refreshing was his sleep.

The sun was shining through the windows when he awoke, strong and healthy. None of his servants had yet returned, because they all thought he was dead. But the nightingale was still sitting there, singing.

'You must stay with me forever,' said the Emperor. 'You shall only sing when you want to, and I will smash the mech-anical bird into a thousand pieces.'

'Don't do that,' said the nightingale. 'It has done the best it could. Keep it as you always have. I can't live in the palace, but let me come whenever I wish. Then in the evening I will sit on the branch by your window and sing for you, to make you both joyous and pensive. I will sing about those who are happy and those who suffer. I will sing about the evil and the good that is kept hidden from you. The little song-bird flies far and wide, to the poor fisherman, to the farmer's rooftop, to everyone who is far from you and your court. I love your heart more than your crown, and yet the crown has a scent of something sacred about it. I will come, I will sing for you. But one thing you must promise me.'

'Anything!' said the Emperor, standing there in his imperial robes, which he had donned himself, and holding the sword that was heavy with gold pressed to his heart.

'One thing I ask of you. Tell no one that you have a little bird who tells you everything, and things will go even better.'

And then the nightingale flew off.

The servants came in to tend to their dead Emperor. Oh yes, there they stood. And the Emperor said, 'Good morning!'

The Red Shoes

There was a little girl who was so delicate and charming, but in the summer she always had to go barefoot because she was poor. In the winter she wore big wooden clogs that made her little ankles turn quite red, and that was awful.

In the middle of the village lived old Mother Shoemaker. She sat and sewed as best she could, using old strips of red cloth to make a little pair of shoes. Quite clumsy they were, but well-intended, and the little girl was to have them. The little girl's name was Karen.

On the very day that her mother was buried, Karen was given the red shoes, and she wore them for the first time. Now, it's true that they weren't the proper shoes for mourning, but she didn't have any others, and so she wore them on her bare feet, walking behind the humble coffin made of straw.

All at once a grand old carriage appeared, and inside sat a grand old woman. She looked at the little girl and felt sorry for her. Then she said to the pastor, 'Listen here, give me that little girl and I will be kind to her!'

Karen thought she said this because of her red shoes, but the old woman said they were awful, and they were burned, while Karen was dressed in nice, clean clothes. She had to learn to read and sew, and people said that she was charming, but the mirror said, 'You are much more than charming, you're lovely!'

Then the queen happened to travel through the land, and she brought along her little daughter, who was a princess. People came flocking to the palace, and Karen was there too. The little princess stood in a window for all to see dressed in fine white clothes. She wore neither a train nor a golden crown, but she had lovely, red kidskin shoes. Of course they were much prettier than the ones that Mother Shoemaker had sewn for little Karen. But nothing in the world could compare with red shoes!

Then Karen was old enough to be confirmed. She was given new clothes and she was also to have new shoes. The rich shoemaker in town measured her little foot. This was at home in his own parlor, where big glass cupboards stood filled with elegant shoes and shiny boots. Everything looked charming, but the old woman didn't see well, so it gave her no pleasure. In the midst of all the shoes stood a pair of red ones just like the ones the princess had worn. How beautiful they were! The shoemaker said they had been sewn for the child of a count, but they didn't fit properly.

'They must be made of the finest leather,' said the old woman. 'How they shine!'

'Yes, how they shine!' said Karen. And they fit, so they were bought. But the old woman didn't know that they were red, because she would never have allowed Karen to be confirmed wearing red shoes, and yet she did.

Everyone looked at her feet. When she walked up the church aisle toward the chancel doorway, she thought even the old paintings on the crypts, those portraits of pastors and their wives wearing stiff collars and long black gowns, had fixed their eyes on her red shoes. And that was all she could think of when the pastor placed his hand on her head and spoke of the holy baptism, of the pact with God, and the fact that she should now be a good Christian. The organ played so solemnly, the children sang so beautifully, and the old cantor sang too, but Karen thought only of her red shoes.

By that afternoon the old woman had heard from everyone that the shoes were red, and she said how dreadful that was. It wasn't the least bit proper. From that day on, whenever Karen went to church, she would always wear black shoes, even if they were old.

The following Sunday was her first communion, and Karen looked at the black shoes, she looked at the red ones – and then she looked at the red ones again and put them on.

It was lovely sunny weather. Karen and the old woman walked along the path through the grain fields where it was rather dusty.

At the church door stood an old soldier with a crutch and a long, odd-looking beard that was more red than white; in fact, it was red. He bowed all the way to the ground and asked the old woman whether he might wipe off her shoes. Karen stretched out her little foot too. 'Oh look, what lovely dancing shoes!' said the soldier. 'Stay on tight when you dance!' Then he slapped his hand on the soles.

The old woman gave the soldier a little *skilling* and then went with Karen into the church.

Everyone inside looked at Karen's red shoes; all the paintings looked at them too. And when Karen knelt before the altar and put the golden chalice to her lips, she thought only of the red shoes. They seemed to be swimming around in the chalice before her, and she forgot to sing the hymn, she forgot to say the Lord's Prayer.

Then everyone left the church, and the old woman climbed into her carriage. As Karen lifted her foot to climb in after her, the old soldier who was standing close by said, 'Oh look, what lovely dancing shoes!' And Karen couldn't help herself, she had to take a few dance steps. As soon as she started, her feet kept on dancing. It was as if the shoes had taken control. She danced around the corner of the church, she couldn't stop herself. The coachman had to run after and grab her, and he lifted her into the carriage, but her feet kept on dancing and she kicked hard at the kind old woman. Finally they managed to take off the shoes, and her feet stopped moving.

At home the shoes were put in a cupboard, but Karen couldn't help looking at them.

Then the old woman fell ill, and they said she wouldn't live long. She needed someone to nurse and tend her, and who should do it but Karen? But over in town there was to be a great ball, and Karen was invited. She looked at the old woman, who didn't have long to live, after all. She looked at the red shoes, and she didn't think there was any sin in that. She put on the red shoes. Why shouldn't she? And then she went to the ball and began to dance.

But when she wanted to turn right, the shoes danced to the left, and when she wanted to move up the floor, the shoes danced down the floor, down the stairs, along the street, and out the town gate. Dance she did, and dance she must, right out into the dark forest.

Then she saw a light overhead among the trees, and she

thought it must be the moon, because it had a face, but it was the old soldier with the red beard. He sat there nodding and said, 'Oh look, what lovely dancing shoes!'

Then Karen was horrified and tried to take off the red shoes, but they wouldn't come off. She tore off her stockings, but the shoes had grown onto her feet; dance she did and dance she must, over field and meadow, in rain and in sunshine, night and day, but nighttime was the most terrible of all.

She danced into the open churchyard, but the dead weren't dancing. They had better things to do than dance. She wanted to sit down on the pauper's grave where bitter tansy grew, but for her there was no peace or rest. And when she danced toward the open church door, she saw an angel there in long white robes, with wings that reached from his shoulders to the ground. His face was stern and solemn, and in his hand he held a sword, gleaming and wide.

'Dance you shall!' he said. 'Dance in your red shoes until you turn pale and cold! Until your skin shrivels up like a mummy's! Dance from door to door. And wherever proud and vain children live, you will knock so they hear and fear you! Dance you shall, dance–!'

'Have mercy!' cried Karen. But she didn't hear what the angel replied, because her shoes carried her through the gate, out to the field, across the road, and along the path, and always she had to keep dancing.

Early one morning she danced past a door she knew quite well. Inside a hymn could be heard, and they carried out a coffin that was adorned with flowers. Then she knew that the old woman was dead, and she felt as if she had now been forsaken by everyone and cursed by the angel of God.

Dance she did, and dance she must, dance into the dark night. Her shoes carried her over thickets and stumps, her feet were worn bloody. She danced across the heath to a lonely little house. She knew that this was where the executioner lived. She tapped her finger on the windowpane and said, 'Come out! Come out! I can't come inside, because I'm dancing!'

And the executioner said, 'Don't you know who I am? I chop off the heads of evil people, and I can feel my ax is trembling!'

'Don't chop off my head,' said Karen. 'Because then I won't be able to repent my sin. But chop off my feet with the red shoes!'

Then she confessed to her sin, and the executioner chopped off her feet with the red shoes. But the shoes kept dancing with the little feet across the fields and into the deep forest.

And he carved wooden feet and crutches for her, taught her a hymn that sinners always sing, and she kissed the hand that had wielded the ax and set out across the heath.

'Now I've suffered enough for those red shoes,' she said. 'Now I'm going to church so they can see me.' And she walked as fast as she could toward the church door, but when she got there, the red shoes were dancing in front of her. She was horrified and turned away.

All week long she was sad and wept many bitter tears, but when Sunday came, she said, 'All right! Now I've suffered and struggled enough! I should think that I'm just as good as many of those people sitting so proudly inside the church.' Then she set off quite boldly, but she got no farther than to the gate when she saw the red shoes dancing in front of her. She was horrified and turned away, repenting her sin with all her heart.

She went over to the parsonage and asked if she might be taken into service there. She would work hard and do everything she could. She had no wish for wages; all she asked for was a roof over her head and permission to stay with good people. The pastor's wife felt sorry for her and gave her a position. And she was hardworking and thoughtful. Quietly she would sit and listen when the pastor read aloud from the Bible in the evening. All the children were very fond of her, but whenever they spoke of adornments and finery and being as lovely as a queen, she would shake her head.

The next Sunday they all went to church and they asked if she would like to come along, but with tears in her eyes she looked sadly at her crutches. Then the others went to hear God's Word while she went alone into her tiny room. It was only big enough for a bed and a chair. There she sat with her hymnbook. As she began reading with a pious heart, the wind carried the tones of the organ from the church to her. She raised her tear-stained face and said, 'Oh, help me, God!'

Then the sun shone so bright, and right in front of her stood the angel of God in the white robes, the one she had seen that night at the church door. He was no longer holding a sharp sword but a lovely green bough that was covered with roses. He touched it to the ceiling, which raised up high, and at the spot he had touched shone a golden star. He touched the walls and they moved outward. She saw the organ that was playing; she saw the old paintings of the pastors and their wives. The congregation was sitting in the carved pews and singing from their hymnals.

The church itself had come home to the poor girl in the tiny, cramped room, or perhaps she had gone to the church. She was sitting in a pew with the others from the parsonage. When they finished the hymn and looked up, they nodded and said, 'It was right for you to come, Karen.'

'It was God's mercy,' she said.

The organ soared, and the children's voices in the choir sounded gentle and lovely. The bright, warm sunshine streamed through the window, reaching the church pew where Karen sat. Her heart was so filled with sunlight, with peace and joy, that it burst. Her soul flew on the sunlight to God, and no one asked about the red shoes.